About the Authors

Having been raised with Scottie, a brother with disabilities, sisters Kaela and Shannon Green developed a passion for teaching inclusion to children at a young age. Kaela and Shannon want to use their love for writing as a forum to educate relationship building with those who are marginalized. Kaela works as a Project Manager in the Medical industry and Shannon is a Special Education Teacher through Teach for America.

Scottie on the Space Station

Kaela C. Green & Shannon E. Green

Scottie on the Space Station

Olympia Publishers
London

www.olympiapublishers.com
OLYMPIA PAPERBACK EDITION

A CIP catalogue record for this title is available from the British Library.

ISBN: 978-1-78830-755-0

First Published in 2020

Olympia Publishers
Tallis House
2 Tallis Street
London
EC4Y 0AB

Printed in Great Britain

Dedication

To Scottie - Thank you for showing us how to view the universe in a different light.

My name is Elli! I am six years old and my family lives on the space station.

I have a little brother named Scottie and a baby sister named Nova.

We get to live in the best place in the universe because Daddy is a scientist and Mommy is a doctor!

Daddy studies the ever-changing galaxies, while Mommy treats sick station workers and any aliens that may need her help.

We even get to meet some of the interesting aliens that visit. They can seem a bit different at first...

But that makes life on the station all the more fun!

My family is used to different because Scottie is a person with disabilities!

Scottie's muscles and brain work in a different way,

so he uses technology to talk and a wheelchair to move around.

Some things are a bit more difficult for Scottie and
he sometimes needs some extra help,

but we still do everything together!

Scottie loves swinging at the park, swimming at the station pool, watching superhero movies,

and chowing down on my Mommy's yummy meatloaf. Just like me!

Some people aren't used to kids with disabilities
like Scottie and that can make me really sad.

But it's just because they don't know him yet, so I introduce him!

One time a little alien came to the station because his sister,

Cosma, needed to get her shots from my mommy.

His name was Junpei and he was six as well!

He was nervous for his sister so Mommy asked me to play with him to keep him company while she worked.

I, of course, introduced him to Scottie and Nova. He thought Nova was the cutest little baby, but he didn't talk much to Scottie.

I took them all to the station's park so we could get some swing and slide time in,

but Junpei still wasn't talking to Scottie.

I decided to ask Junpei,

"Why won't you talk to my brother?"

Junpei looked down at his feet and embarrassedly said,

"I want to, but I just don't know what to say."

This I understood, sometimes I don't even know what to say to new people!

I tried to think of something they might have in common.

"Oh Junpei! You can talk to Scottie about whatever you want and he'd be so excited!

I want breakfast

Superhero movies are my favorite

His tablet allows him to talk about anything, even superheroes!"

"His body may look and work a little differently than ours do,

but he still enjoys some of the same things and wants new friends!"

Junpei looked down at his feet and whispered,

"Scottie also loves superheroes?"

Scottie, speaking with his tablet said,

"I love superheroes! Especially the ones that flyyyyy!"

Junpei looked up to Scottie and said excitedly,

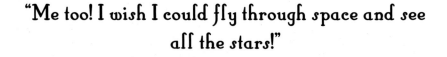

"Me too! I wish I could fly through space and see all the stars!"

We all giggled and talked about what exciting
superpowers we would have.

Scottie would be our flier and I would travel through time!

Junpei would have super speed.

Nova would be content just learning to walk and talk.

Then Mommy walked into the park

with Junpei's entire family!

Junpei ran to his sister and exclaimed, "I want you to meet my friend Scottie!

He is a human boy with disabilities, but he loves superheroes like me! We are pretending he can fly!"

His sister's face lit up.

"Oh wow! Hi Scottie! Can I play too? I can have super strength!"

"Scottie smiled brightly, clicked a few buttons on his tablet, and said,

"Great choice! My friends and I could really use someone who has super-strength to help us battle the incoming space monsters!"